FIRE FIGHT

Jacqueline Guest

7th Generation
Summertown, Tennessee

Library of Congress Cataloging-in-Publication Data

Guest, Jacqueline.
Fire fight / Jacqueline Guest.
    pages cm
  ISBN 978-1-939053-11-4 (pbk.) -- ISBN 978-1-939053-98-5 (e-book)
  1. Navajo Indians--Alberta--Fiction. 2. Assiniboine Indians--Alberta--
Fiction. [1. Navajo Indians--Fiction. 2. Assiniboine Indians--Fiction. 3.
Indians of North America--Alberta. 4. Runaways--Fiction. 5. Identity--
Fiction. 6. Alberta--Fiction. 7. Canada--Fiction.] I. Title.
  PZ7.G938175Fi 2015
  [Fic]--dc23

                                2015007693

7th Generation
an imprint of Book Publishing Company
PO Box 99
Summertown, TN 38483
888-260-8458
bookpubco.com

ISBN: 978-1-939053-11-4

20 19 18 17 16 15   1 2 3 4 5 6 7 8 9

Printed in the United States

Book Publishing Company is a
member of Green Press Initiative.
We chose to print this title on paper
with 100% postconsumer recycled
content, processed without chlorine,
which saved the following natural
resources:
• 18 trees
• 563 pounds of solid waste
• 8,414 gallons of water
• 1,551 pounds of greenhouse gases
• 8 million BTUs of energy

For more information on
Green Press Initiative, visit
greenpressinitiative.org.
Environmental impact estimates
were made using the Environmental
Defense Fund Paper Calculator.
For more information visit
papercalculator.org.

Contents

I stared down into the still face of death, hardly recognizing the lifeless shell lying in the coffin. This was the worst day of my entire sixteen years on this planet.

My *ikusin*, my grandmother, was the most important person in my life, and now she was gone. I was alone, which meant Stoney Nakoda Social Services would come calling . . . again. They knew me as a "born troublemaker"— their words, not mine—and would toss me into foster care until I was an *adult* of eighteen. Right. As if you could put a number on that.

Or worse. They'd send me to the States to live with my Navajo relatives, whom I've never met! The only thing Navajo about me is my first name, Kai. It means "willow tree," and my parents chose it because of the willows around our house, where I was born.

The name Kai Hunter is a mash-up, like me—part Navajo, part Stoney Nakoda. My parents met on the powwow trail, married, and stayed here on the Stoney Reserve near Calgary, Alberta. We were a happy, normal family. All of that came to a fiery end one rainy night when a drunk driver ran my parents' car off the road. They both died, and I moved in with my grandmother. And now . . .

I touched Gran's cold hand, still trying to wrap my head around her really being dead. "Thanks for taking such good care of her, Mr. One Spot." I smiled weakly at the undertaker.

"Be back at eleven for the service, Kai. Mrs. Wesley's arranged a full ceremony, complete with a smudge and an honor song, and there's going to be a mighty fine round dance. The elders say the spirit of your *ikusin* will be at the dance."

I nodded mutely, knowing this was my final good-bye. Gran's send-off sounded amazing. Wish I could be there.

At home, I stuffed my few belongings into a backpack and strapped it to my ancient '74 ME-125 Indian motorcycle. I already had my most important possession—my mother's locket. Gran had received it from her mother on her wedding day and given it to my mum when she married dad. I got it this year on my birthday because Gran said she wasn't going to be here for my wedding day. I'll always wonder how she'd known.

A dust cloud far down the road caught my attention. Shading my eyes from the hot August sun, I tried to make out who was coming. With a jolt, I recognized the cars—it was the tribal police, and right behind them, social services. Man, they weren't wasting any time.

I yanked on my helmet and goggles. My old bike was a moody hag and often chose the worst time to show me she was boss, like now. I kicked and kicked, but the stubborn thing wouldn't start.

I could see the cars getting closer. "Come on. If you start, I'll buy you a fresh can of oil. You know, the good kind you like."

The cars turned onto my road. They'd be here in less than a minute.

With a chain smoker's cough, the engine finally turned over and grudgingly caught. "Thanks, you old pirate queen!" Tires spinning, I headed off-road, into the hills.

Cutting through the bush, I tried to figure out what to do. So far, my master plan consisted of staying out of the authorities' gunsights. Beyond that, I had nothing.

When I came to the Trans-Canada Highway, it was decision time: east or west? East would take me to Calgary, a city large enough that I could easily hide out in the concrete jungle. Going west, I'd eventually end up in Vancouver, an even bigger city. It had so many runaways, what was one more? The problem was, I'd be a target for every pimp, drug dealer, or low life, who'd spot a teen on the run in a heartbeat.

There was another option.

Banff, Alberta, high in the Rocky Mountains, was only forty-five minutes west. It was a friendly little town filled with tourists and other people just passing through. I could disappear into the crowd until I came up with a plan. No one would expect me to be hiding in plain sight so close to home.

With one last glance over my shoulder, I turned west.

CHAPTER TWO
Duck and Cover

The first thing I did in Banff was find a drugstore. Next, I went to a service station and asked to use the washroom. The pimply-faced gas jockey gave me a hard time and wouldn't give me the key. What a jerk.

My small pool of patience instantly drained away. I gave him a laser glare that said I wasn't screwing around, and if he wanted to come out of this breathing, he wouldn't mess with me. The gutless wonder shrank down to the size of the toad he was and handed over the key. In my book, he went from a jerk to a wimp.

Staring at the mirror, I wondered where to start. If I wanted to pass as an ordinary citizen and not a girl running for her life, changes had to be made.

The overall picture was okay: one hundred and ten pounds, five foot four, athletic build, and wide-set eyes that could size you up in a heartbeat. Nature had done okay; it was my additions that made me so distinctive. They'd been cool, but now they were a liability.

The piercings had to go. I took off all but a single pair of my earrings, and I had four holes in each ear. That left two rings in my eyebrow and a cute little nose stud I'd picked up at this year's Tsuu T'ina powwow. I removed them all.

Next, my wrist tattoo. That was a problem. A tat is a lot easier to get than it is to get rid of. The bandage I'd bought would cover the beautiful dragonfly for now. Later I could buy an awesome cuff or wide bracelet to hide it.

The last thing was the toughest. I inherited my best feature, my Navajo hair, from my mother. Thick, black, and glossy; it reached to my waist. As I raised the scissors, I turned away from the mirror. I couldn't watch.

When it was done, I felt terrible, as if I wasn't a Stoney Nakoda girl anymore. Carefully, I tucked my long, severed braid into my backpack.

Finally, the tricky part. I picked up the box of hair lightener and read the instructions. The lady at the drugstore said it would change my hair to blond and cover all my grays. Who could ask for anything more?

When I finished, I gawked in horror at the reflection in the mirror. Instead of "warm tawny gold" as promised, the girl looking back had "rusted-out orange" hair, perfect for Halloween. Great! I was trying to blend in, and now I stuck out like a stoplight.

Someone hammering on the door signaled that my time was up. Cursing, I grabbed my backpack and left.

According to a travel brochure I picked up, Banff was a "gem cradled in the embrace of the Rockies, famous for its hot springs and mountain views." There sure were plenty of tourists from all over the world. The place was jammed. I saw lots of twenty-somethings in shorts and hiking boots, their packs loaded for roughing it.

This gave me an idea. Turning my bike onto Wolf Street, I kept going, first to Tunnel Mountain, then to Hidden Ridge Way. There it was: The Banff Mountain Hostel, a haven for weary, young travelers with little money.

A slim, thirty-something woman greeted me at the reception desk. "Hello, *bonjour*, and welcome. Can I help you?" she asked with a smile, not giving my glowing orange hair so much as a blink.

"How much is a room?" It came out with an icy edge of teen attitude.

The smiling woman didn't seem to notice. "Dorm room is thirty-nine."

My stomach sank. I'd brought all the money I had: one hundred and ninety bucks. But at that rate, camping in the bush was in my near future. Maybe I'd treat myself tonight. Tomorrow, I'd buy a cheap sleeping bag to call home.

"One night."

I admit, my hand trembled the tiniest bit as I pulled two twenties from my beaded wallet.

The woman eyed me closely. "You know, I'm sorry, I didn't get your name."

Another detail I hadn't covered. I'd need an alias in case the cops came calling. Glancing out the window, I saw a bird on the lawn. "Robin! Robin . . . Pearce!" I blurted, recalling the last name of the heroine in the book I was reading.

She paused for a moment. "Well, Robin Pearce, as it happens, one of my pub staff quit yesterday, and I'm in need of a replacement. It's minimum wage, plus tips. You'd also get a free room in the staff quarters." She laughed. "I guess I should ask if you'd be interested in the job before giving you the spiel."

A lot of things ran through my mind. I wasn't sticking around Banff. However, while I was here, it wouldn't hurt to make some money. And having a dry place to sleep, away from bears and cougars, was a deal clincher. "Yeah, a job would be great! I arrived from Vancouver today and was going to find work right after I checked in." The lie slid easily off my tongue.

"Do you have any experience working in a restaurant?"

It was a simple question, yet somehow I knew my answer was important.

"To be honest, not much."

This was the truth. I'd worked one shift at the Nakoda Lodge and been fired. The boss said it was a clash of personalities—mine sucked, and he couldn't stand me. I hurriedly smoothed over this.

"I promise I'm a quick learner and a hard worker." The renewed smile on the woman's face told me I'd passed the test.

"I didn't think you were the waitress type. Let's give it a couple of weeks to see if we're a good fit." She came around the counter and handed me back my twenties. "I'm Anne Collier, the manager here. Welcome aboard, Robin."

As I shook her hand, I noticed the discoloration around my fingernails. Guess I should have worn gloves when I ruined my hair. "I appreciate the job..." I searched for something appropriate to call her. "... Ms. Collier."

"It's Mrs., but Anne is fine. Come on, I'll take you to the staff quarters, and after that, we'll do the paperwork. I'll need some official ID, like a driver's license, for proof of age. Working at the Root Cellar, our world-famous pub," she added proudly, "means you'd be serving alcohol."

Without missing a beat, another lie rocketed off my lips. "Actually, I was robbed in Surrey on my way here. It was really scary. The scum had a knife and got everything, including my wallet with all my ID." I was shocked at how good I was at thinking up total crap on the spot.

She motioned for me to follow her. "Did the police catch the guy?"

"Not a chance." I said with the perfect amount of indignation. "The cops couldn't care less about one girl getting robbed." I thought of all the tips bar waitresses get and added, "No worries, though. I'm totally eighteen."

"We'll have to start you in the hostel's restaurant, Cougar Jack's, where there's no alcohol, until you get some ID. Oh, and I forgot to tell you another job perk," Anne continued. "Staff get one meal per shift free, usually supper, and I'll throw in breakfast too. Do you have enough money to carry you through to payday?" She eyed the two twenties I still clutched tightly.

"Yeah, I'm good." I hastily jammed the bills into my wallet.

"Why don't you take the rest of today off to explore Banff? It's a great town." She passed me the key to my room.

"Thanks, uh . . . Anne."

After hauling my stuff into my room—which turned out to be small, clean, and decorated in a wild-woods style with a log bed and braided rugs—I headed out for a leisurely afternoon. Life was sweet. I thought of how proud Gran would have been about me scoring a job in the first fifteen minutes of arriving in town.

Thinking of Gran made a wave of sadness wash over me. Maybe not everything was sweet.

The afternoon was hot, and for once, my old bike performed well. I went to see the usual tourist attractions—frothing Bow Falls, the Upper Hot Springs (which smelled of sulfur), and the Cave and Basin, where prospectors in 1883 found the original hot springs. Their discovery led to the establishment of Canada's first national park—and Banff is at the center of it. Although I'd seen it all before, pretending to be a tourist was kinda cool.

As evening shadows crept over the valley, I decided it was time for supper and started back to the hostel. The thought of a hot meal made my mouth water. I hadn't eaten since early that morning, before I said good-bye to Gran. It would have been nice to be at her ceremony.

I'm sure she understood I had no choice except to bail.

I'd turned onto Wolf Street when suddenly a rusted green step-side pickup barreled through the red light. It was in the intersection before I had the chance to process what was happening.

Reflexes took over and I cranked on the throttle to get out of the way. True to her miserable nature, that old bike didn't respond. The massive truck grill loomed in front of me.

I had nowhere to go!

CHAPTER THREE
Superhero in Coveralls

A split second before the crash, I leaped off the bike and rolled across the pavement.

The truck hit the motorcycle, sending it crashing into the curb. I clambered to my feet in time to see the pickup rocketing down the street. I noticed one taillight was busted, and the bare bulb glared at me as the truck disappeared.

"You jerk!" I shouted, more angry than hurt. As I scanned the mangled mess that was left of my old Indian, all I could think of was the repair bill.

"Man, that stinks!"

The voice made me whirl around. Without warning, I was captivated by glacier-blue eyes and a grease-smudged face.

"I saw you take your header. You okay?"

Frowning, I refocused. I didn't want this do-gooder calling an ambulance, or worse, the cops. I nudged the broken mirror with my boot. "Yeah, I'm good. It's my bike that needs the paramedics. This really bites." I could feel tears threatening and blinked. This was no time to get all weepy. "I bet there aren't any parts in all of Banff to fix this old wreck."

The guy grinned lazily. "I might be able to help."

It was then I noticed the coveralls with "Ace Auto Repairs" stitched on a patch and "Rory" in flowing script underneath.

"You a mechanic or something?"

"Or something." He flashed me his killer smile again. "I work at the garage across the street. We do car repairs, and in my spare time, I twist wrenches on bikes." He crouched down and inspected the wreckage, picking up a mangled piece. "I've got to admit, I haven't seen one like this before. What is it?"

"About a million years ago, it started out as an Indian Enduro. It's been fixed and rebuilt so many times, there's nothing much left of the original bike except the decal."

He tossed the remnant onto the ground, then wiggled the carburetor. "You're right. Not many parts for this old beast around here. I might have some substitutes at my place." He hefted the bashed-up machine onto its wheels and started pushing it up Wolf Street. "The name's Rory Adams."

I thought of my new persona. "Robin Pearce." I trailed behind, picking up parts as they fell off the bike.

By the time he wheeled up a nearby driveway and into a wooden garage, I had my arms full of bits and pieces of what used to be my motorcycle. I dumped everything onto the workbench. Turning, I saw a gleaming KTM 690 Enduro sitting proudly in the corner of the garage.

"Wow!" I whispered. "She's a beauty." I walked over, reciting the specs I knew by heart. "Sixty-eight horsepower, electric starter, six speed, claw-shifted tranny, APTC anti-hopping clutch."

"You know your stuff. I'm impressed." There was a note of respect in Rory's voice.

I liked that note. When it came to my crazy passion for bikes, I usually got dumped on. "Yeah. I'm kinda into two-wheels."

"You're the first girl I've met who knows what an awesome ride I have. Very cool."

"Very cool," I agreed, feeling my face blush.

I don't handle praise well. I'm not used to it.

Rory and I spent the next hour figuring out what had to be fixed and what could wait. I told him about coming from Vancouver, staying at the hostel and waitressing at the restaurant, and how I hoped to eventually work at the Root Cellar. He told me he was eighteen, had no family alive, was working at getting his mechanic's certification, and that he rented this house with two buddies.

Finally, after going over all the busted and broken guts on my bike, we had a list of the most essential items.

"Man, this is going to cost a mint." The words caught in my throat.

I jumped as three guys burst into the garage, laughing and talking.

"Hey, Rory, my man, we need some Monday night party fixin's and—"

They stopped short when they saw me.

"Robin, this is Kyle and Rat, my roommates, and Jimbo. Guys, this fine young thing had a bit of a crash-o-dent, and I'm fixing her bike for her."

"Sure, just fixing her bike." The one called Kyle sniggered.

Rory glared, and Kyle shut up. "You deadbeats wait here. I'll take Robin up to the hostel. Be back in half an hour."

Rat snorted skeptically. "Half an hour for a ten-minute ride?"

"Some things are too good to rush." Rory shrugged out of his coveralls, revealing a sleeveless T-shirt underneath.

I couldn't help noticing the gun show—the guy's muscles actually rippled! Gran would say, "the Great Spirit spoiled him." I slid my battered helmet on and tried not to stare.

Rory, I saw, had a high-end Arai motocross helmet tricked out with navy-and-gold graphics. When he started the KTM, the single-cylinder four-stroke made the walls shake. I could feel the engine vibration through the seat of my pants as I sat behind him, holding on extra tight.

We fit together really well.

CHAPTER FOUR
Invite to the Prom

Instead of rushing off, Rory sat with me on the steps of the staff quarters and we chatted about what I did back in Vancouver, which required more fast thinking. I said I worked as a clerk in a store before quickly switching the topic to him. "How about you? Are you from Banff?"

"Nah, I've only been here a few months. I don't know how long I'll stay." He turned his thousand-watt smile on me. "Though I gotta say, now that you're here, I could be persuaded to stick around."

He was so friendly; I was really flattered. I didn't want him to leave and tried to stall him. "Um, thanks . . . for the ride."

"No big deal." He lit a cigarette, then flicked the lit match away.

I watched it land in a pile of grass clippings. There was a brief flare before it went out. "Careful, the grass is dry." It would be typical of my luck if the place burned down before I'd even had my free meal.

He blew a perfect smoke ring and I stuck my finger into the middle of it. "I've always wanted to do that." I laughed.

"You're something." His eyes slid over me and I shivered. "How about going to a party with me Saturday night?"

I was so surprised, I didn't know what to say. I wasn't exactly Miss Popularity back on the rez. This gorgeous guy was asking me out and with my new flame-orange, jaggedly hacked hair, I could hardly be called runway ready.

My new job popped into my head. My lousy luck was holding. I'm finally asked on a date and have to worry about a stupid, minimum-wage, no-brainer job! I felt light-headed with excitement but had to be cool. "Sure, if I have the night off." I used my because-I'm-so-bored-I'll-let-you-take-me-out voice.

Rory stood and bowed gallantly. "Pick you up at eight."

He left and I heard his thumper roar off as I walked into Cougar Jack's, the hostel's restaurant. I must admit, I was smiling. So much that my face hurt.

"Robin! Over here!"

Anne Collier waved from a back table and it took me a second to realize she was talking to me, Robin Pearce. I joined her, reminding myself of all the fake personal details I'd given her.

"Did you enjoy your afternoon?" she asked, handing me a menu.

My mind filled with images of the bike crash and Rory Adams. "Apart from one little hiccup, I really did."

"I've got your work schedule." Anne read the sheet on the table in front of her. "You'll start here in Cougar Jack's with the morning shift, six thirty until one thirty. It will give you a chance to learn the ropes."

The thought of schlepping to the restaurant at the crack of dawn made me want to groan. "I'd rather work at the Root Cellar." I knew tips in the bar would be way better.

"Until you can prove you're eighteen, I can't take a chance. If a liquor inspector came in, it would cost me my license."

I knew better than to push things. I didn't want to raise any suspicions. "Yeah, sure, I understand." One good thing about the schedule from hell was that I would have a big part of the day free and—bonus!—I could go out with Rory on Saturday.

Supper was a delicious Fat Cat burger and a side of French fries covered with brown gravy and cheese called *poutine*. As I ate, Anne told me more about the job and gave me my uniforms, two black shirts with a small Cougar Jack's logo on the pocket. When she shifted to more personal stuff, I knew it was time to get out of there.

"Thanks for the meal. I gotta go." I was about to leave when a tall, dark-haired man with a deep tan walked over. I noticed that his work clothes were dirty and there was soot on his face. He smelled strongly of smoke.

"Robin, this is Mike, my husband." Anne eyed him and wrinkled her nose. "He's a rapattack hero, and from what I see, he had a hot time at work."

"You'd be right." Mike pulled a chair out and sat down. "There was a little problem up on the Smith Dorrien Trail. Some idiot in a truck lights a campfire and drives away. Poof! Next thing you know, the guys and I are earning our paychecks again."

He laughed, a deep rumbling sound that made me feel happy. "What's a rapattack hero?" I hoped I didn't sound too ignorant, but I'd never heard the term.

Mike turned to me. "It's short for 'rapid attack,' and the 'hero' part is optional. I work for the Alberta Forestry Service. When a fire starts, a rapattack crew is helicoptered in. We rappel down to the forest floor and put the fire out before it has a chance to turn into something big. In some places, they call us smoke jumpers."

"It sounds exciting." And it did. I couldn't imagine flying around zapping forest fires for a living.

"It can be," he agreed. "We like it better if the excitement's kept to a dull roar. How do you know Anne?"

"She hired me to be part of the waitstaff here." I'd been about to leave, but now I had to stay. I wanted to know more about this rapattack stuff. "Join us?"

Mike inspected his filthy clothes. "I'm not really dressed for dining out, but if you ladies don't mind, I haven't had anything since breakfast and I could eat a bear."

Anne rolled her eyes. "Fine. Just sit downwind of me."

Mike spent the next hour talking about firefighting. By the time dessert rolled around, I was hooked. It was the kind of thing they should make into an action movie.

"Who wouldn't want a job like yours? It must be wicked to do all that stuff!" I was truly impressed.

Mike finished his coffee. "Well, sure. But it's not for everyone. You have to be in really good physical shape and be able to go at a moment's notice. If some other jurisdiction needs us, we work for them, no matter how far from home. Conditions aren't soft. It's tough, dirty, and dangerous."

His passion was addictive and I listened, mesmerized.

"It's also worth it, Robin. Stopping a forest fire is an incredible achievement. It can make you feel—"

"Like a rapattack hero," Anne finished the sentence for him as she leaned over to plant a kiss on his soot-covered cheek.

"Your job is totally interesting and exciting and cool!" I was babbling, and both Mike and Anne laughed.

Anne teased her husband. "I think you have a fan."

"Hey, I can't help it if the lady has good taste."

Mike winked at me and I found myself winking back. It was then I knew I had to get out of there. This wasn't me. I didn't do warm and fuzzy. "I'd best be going. Early day tomorrow. I don't want to be late for my first shift."

"Smart thinking," Mike agreed. "I hear your boss is tough."

"Don't scare her off. I'm short staffed as it is!" Anne slapped him playfully on the arm.

I grabbed my shirts and walked out feeling like I was leaving the party early.

CHAPTER FIVE
Party Time

Work was an education. I discovered that being a waitress was a lot harder and took a lot more smarts than I'd thought. I had to carefully write every order down (including all the annoying "special changes" the customers wanted). I also had to mop up a million spills, clean slimy tables, keep cranky kids quiet with crayons, figure out the complicated till, and deliver the food hot and to the right table. And I needed to do it all while smiling and making cutesy conversation so I'd get a decent tip!

By the time my shifts were over, I'd be so tired that I usually ended up napping before supper. The other staff were real friendly and I worried about getting too chummy, in case I messed up and let some personal detail slip.

Another benefit of the staff quarters was the laundry facilities. They were coin operated, so my tips came in handy. With so few clothes, I used the washer a lot and would hang stuff to dry. There was a ceiling fan in my room, and I'd tie the wet laundry to a line attached to the fan blades. My delicates would whirl around like flying demons, drying in no time, and I didn't have to spend precious money on the machine dryer. I had to remember the flying demons when I got up during the night, of course, or else a wet pair of socks would attack me. I thought my airborne clothesline was genius.

Saturday rolled around, and by the end of my shift, I wondered if Rory had remembered our date. He hadn't called. I went to my room and slept until nearly seven, waking up equal parts ticked off and disappointed. Rory Adams was all smoke and mirrors.

Then I heard it. The rumble of his bike outside launched a squadron of dragonflies in my stomach.

I'd borrowed a colorful scarf and tied it around my neck to offset my worn jean jacket. The girl in the mirror wouldn't pass for eighteen, so I undid an extra button on my blouse. Better. Wetting my hair, I tried to arrange the chopped orange mess as though it was a new style done on purpose. Nothing helped, though, so I gave up and raced outside.

"Wow! Baby girl, the word for you is *hot*! Ready to party?" Rory revved his bike. He had on a navy-and-white leather jacket that matched his helmet. I knew what was underneath the jacket and decided he was truly an impressive package.

Suddenly, I felt nervous. Rory thought I was eighteen, and his friends were a little out there. Okay, a *lot* out there. I shook it off. Being paranoid wouldn't help my love life. "Party is my middle name," I bragged, hoping I could live up to the billing.

We rode toward Lake Louise. It was a beautiful night, and Rory pushed his bike full out. Several times he blasted past cars, narrowly missing a collision with oncoming traffic. The guy was an adrenalin junkie, and I found it thrilling. We hurtled through the mountains, me hanging on to his waist and loving the feel of his body so close to mine.

When we arrived, the campground was filled with partygoers waving beer bottles in the air. Rory parked, and when he took off his jacket he revealed a form-fitting, crimson polo shirt underneath. It skimmed over every muscle. Nice.

"Come on, baby girl. I'll introduce you."

He led me to the fire. "You already know these three degenerates." He nodded toward Kyle, Jimbo, and Rat, who'd obviously started the party hours ago.

"Hi," I said lamely.

"Jeez, the big man brought his Injun princess." Kyle slurred.

I stiffened.

"Her name is Robin, you loser." There was no mistaking Rory's harsh tone.

"He didn't mean anything, man." Rat said, defending his wasted buddy.

Jimbo tossed a bottle to Rory, then offered me one. "Maybe the princess wants a beer?"

"Keep the 'princess' part and we'll get along fine," I snapped, taking the beer.

"Whoa! I guess she told us!" Kyle snorted.

Rory draped his arm around my shoulders. "She's working at Cougar Jack's now and will eventually end up at the Root Cellar." This got the attention of the other three.

"You mean she'd have access to the booze?" Kyle asked, interested.

"Why, yes. Yes, she would," Rory answered, like it was some kind of joke.

"Could come in handy on a Saturday night," Rat added, slugging back his beer.

I wasn't sure if they were kidding, but I didn't want Rory to think I was a wet blanket. "Yeah, that's me. OK Liquor: Open 24/7." They all laughed.

"Bottle counts are out all the time in bars. The leprechauns or booze fairies spirit away their share." Rory whispered in my ear, his breath hot. "Once you're in the bar, maybe some of those fairies will show up on your shift."

I was speechless. This guy moved at the speed of light and I felt out of my depth. My mouth opened and shut like a guppy gulping air.

Rory laughed. "Let's mingle."

We joined another group of revelers, which included three girls who must have been about nineteen but who could have passed for thirty with their thick makeup. Who wears false eyelashes to a keg party?

"Ladies, this is Robin. Robin, the ladies." The girls giggled, a trio of mindless Barbies, I was sure.

"Hi," I mumbled. No one could accuse me of being too chatty.

"Why don't you get acquainted? I have to talk to Rat."

Rory left me standing there feeling incredibly awkward, so I drank the beer Jimbo had given me and a second one. I was soon on my third and knew I'd better get some food or I'd be sorry. "How about a hot dog?" I asked.

"Come on. I'll show you where the grub is," said one of the Barbies. I think her name was Twila or Twinkie or something.

"Thanks. I need something solid in my stomach." I could hear a slight slur when I spoke.

It turned out to be Twila. She seemed like she was all right. She gave me the insider scoop on everyone at the party, even Rory.

"Robin, you gotta know our Rory's a player. He's always had an eye for the girls."

"Yeah, I figured. No guy looks that delicious and sings in the choir. It doesn't bother me. The old song says it all: 'I'm here for a good time, not a long time.'"

"You know it." Twila giggled and handed me another beer.

***

The fire burned down and was perfect for toasting marshmallows. I'd finished off four when Rory sauntered over. "Hey, baby girl. Cook me one of those?"

I made him a perfect, golden-brown one and he ate it, licking his fingers. "Sweet. Like you."

He leaned in and kissed me softly, as though he didn't want to break me. His mouth tasted of marshmallows. It was so unexpected. All I could do was stand there, frozen.

"Hey, let's heat up this party!" Rory went to the woodpile and grabbed a couple of logs. When he tossed them onto the fire, a huge shower of sparks rose into the night sky. The glowing ash drifted upward, a thousand tiny fireflies, and landed on the pine trees, flaring for a second before going dark.

"Whooo-wee! What a light show!" Rory threw back his head and howled like a wolf.

The pyrotechnics were spectacular, and I joined him in his salute to the tiny lights. We both laughed as he put his arms around me and kissed me again, this time with as much heat as the crackling sparks we'd watched spiral into the air.

Everything was going well until Jimbo staggered over. "Rory, buddy, how's about we do a little dance in honor of your red-skin princess?"

Lumbering around the fire, he made ridiculous war whoops and pretended to shoot a bow and arrow. It didn't take long before Rat and Kyle joined in, hooting and hollering. Rory laughed at their drunken antics.

I was so embarrassed I wanted to crawl away into the brush.

Finally, Rory smashed his beer bottle against one of the rocks in the circle of stones surrounding the fire. Everyone stopped what they were doing, including the three ignorant dancers. "Show's over, gentlemen."

There was some mumbling before the crowd went back to what they'd been doing. I didn't say anything. Instead, I mentally crossed all three idiots off my Christmas list.

The rest of the night sort of blurred together, until finally it was time to call it quits.

"Let's go, baby girl." Rory motioned toward his bike.

"What about the fire?" It seemed to have burned itself out, but after hearing those stories from Mike, I had to be sure.

"It's fine," Rory assured me. "Robin, a fire is like us; it's alive. It needs three things to exist: something to start it going, oxygen to breathe, and fuel so it can eat." He tossed a small stick into the fire pit. It glowed, caught, and then went out quickly. "Sure, there are embers to ignite it and lots of air, but there's no fuel. All it takes is one of those three things to be missing and a fire will do what we all do; it dies." He sighed impatiently. "Come on. I'm friggin' tired."

I didn't move. Instead, I kept staring at him, with my we-can-do-this-the-hard-way-or-we-can-do-it-my-way face.

"All right, you win!" He turned to the remaining revelers. "Come on, you bunch of drunks. We need a bucket brigade to make sure the fire's out or Smokette the Bear here won't leave."

There were some biker types who obligingly went to the creek and brought back several buckets of water. Judging from the huge cloud of steam gushing from the ashes, the fire hadn't been as close to out as we'd thought.

"Thanks, Rory." I gave his hand a squeeze.

"Anything to keep my girl happy."

His girl! Of all the things he could have said, this was the absolute best. My heart melted.

The long ride home was chilly, and I snuggled in close to Rory's back. The air was fresh with pine scent and the stars, which shone like angels, were lighting the way for us. I could have ridden to the moon with him.

We entered Banff, and I was sad the night was over. The sleepy mountain town was eerily silent in the predawn stillness.

Without warning, the quiet was shattered, and my heart leaped into my throat!

This couldn't be happening!

CHAPTER SIX
Downs and Ups

The wail of a Royal Canadian Mounted Police cruiser's siren shocked me and I jerked upright. The flashing blue-and-red lights made my stomach twist. The RCMP were never a good thing. I heard Rory cursing as he pulled over to the side of the road.

This was bad. I was sixteen, drunk, with an eighteen-year-old guy, *and* I was a runaway, probably a fugitive by now if the tribal police had anything to say about it. I had no ID, and if they wanted to, the Mounties could arrest me, then all my secrets would come spilling out.

When the bike stopped, I climbed off, keeping my goggles on in a kind of semi-disguise. I tried to keep my distance. No sense sharing my beer breath with the officer. Rory swung his leg over the seat, and as he turned, he bumped into me. I was still a little woozy and could feel myself tilting off balance.

Rory reached out and pulled me to him, adding a little squeeze. "Don't worry. Cops are always hassling me."

The officer walked toward us and I tensed.

"Evening, folks. License and registration, please." The constable shone his flashlight on us, stepping closer as he eyed me. I tried for nonchalant, which was about as far from how I felt as you could get.

Rory pulled his helmet off and handed over the documents. "What's the problem, officer?"

I was amazed at how cool he sounded. The cop read the license, compared the picture to Rory's face, scanned the registration, and then gave everything back. "Your taillight's out."

"What? It was working earlier." Rory went to the back of the bike, frowning. "Son of a gun! I'll get it fixed first thing in the morning. Thanks, officer."

"Kind of late to be out." The officer eyed me as he spoke.

Rory had the nerve to chuckle. "Actually, it's kind of early. It was such a nice night for a ride, I guess time got away from us. We're on our way home now."

The constable gave us another once-over. "Be sure to get that taillight fixed, son." He returned to the cruiser, and I let out a breath I hadn't realized I'd been holding.

Helmeted once more, Rory climbed back on the bike. I tucked in behind him, still shaken up.

As we pulled into the parking lot at the hostel, exhaustion flooded me. I climbed off the bike and removed my helmet and goggles as I waited for Rory. I was sure he'd want to kiss me and hoped my breath didn't smell too rank.

He leaped off the bike. "Man, close call or what! You were perfect, baby girl."

Rory moved closer, and I thought he was going to lean in for the big good-night finale. Instead, he reached into my jacket pocket and pulled out a small brown bag.

"It could have been a little dicey if Joe Cop had found this." He stuffed the package into his leather jacket.

A little dicey? Are you kidding?

I was about to protest when Rory put his arms around me. "I had a lot of fun tonight."

This time he did kiss me, and I saw those sparks again. He was a very good kisser.

"See you tomorrow, or more like later today."
He laughed and climbed back on his bike.

I watched him drive away, not sure if I should
be angry or happy. Rory must have slipped the
bag into my pocket when he bumped into me at
the police stop. I had a good idea what was in it
and knew better than to find out. Don't ask, can't
tell. The chances of the cop checking me were
slimmer than for Rory, but if I'd been caught
with the bag, I'd have been in deep trouble. Who
would believe it wasn't mine?

I guess Rory figured that since I was a fine
upstanding citizen, there was no reason the
officer would pat me down. Little did he know.
It was so hard to be angry with him, especially
when I remembered us howling at the moon as
we'd watched those sparks light up the night.

I could see the dawn graying the eastern
sky as I walked into the building. Ahead of me
loomed my long, *long* morning shift.

***

I barely managed to make it through work,
and my lack of tips reflected my low level of
attention to customers. The schedule listed

Monday as my assigned day off. Awesome! I was seriously overdrawn at the sleep bank.

Monday morning I awoke feeling more like my old self. Not that my old self was any screaming wonder, but at least my head didn't threaten to fall off every time I bent over. I was having a cup of coffee at what I'd come to call the staff table in Cougar Jack's when Anne came over.

"Feeling better?" she asked, surprising me. I thought I'd flown under the radar with my poor waitressing skills. "Yesterday, you seemed a little under the weather. I had a couple of complaints."

I had the decency to look guilty. "I'm sorry. It was a touch of the flu. I'm better now."

Yeah, the "alco-flu." I hoped she wouldn't guess that I'd been partying so hard I went straight from buzzed to hungover when I'd come to work, which was just two short hours after Rory and I got back. My new boss was cool and I didn't want to disappoint her. Tensing, I waited for the inevitable lecture.

"Better is good. I'd hate for you to get one of those nasty summer colds."

Not what I'd expected, and for some reason, it made me feel worse for lying to her.

We both looked up as Mike walked in wearing coveralls, boots, a hard hat, and a backpack. All he was missing was his shovel and ax and he could have been auditioning for *Firefighter's Monthly*.

"I thought I'd find the prettiest girls in Banff sitting here." He gave his wife a kiss.

"Don't you have rapattack drills today?" Anne asked.

"We do. I'm here on official business." He grinned mischievously. "We need coffee."

"What kind of drills?" I asked, curious.

"The usual. Jumping out of helicopters, slashing brush, hauling axes and shovels, and of course, digging up all of Alberta with those shovels. Total excitement."

Even though his tone was light, I knew the work was deadly serious. "Do you think I could come and, you know, watch? If it's allowed, I mean."

Mike raised an eyebrow at Anne, who shrugged. "It's her day off. She can do whatever she wants."

"Fine with me. You're in charge of the coffee, Robin."

I jumped up, thrilled to go along. "Sure. How much?"

"How many gallons can you carry?" Mike said with a wink.

We got the coffee and two dozen donuts from the bakery before driving to a deserted fire road east of Canmore, thirty minutes away. I wanted to show off my knowledge and told Mike about a fire being a living thing, needing something to start it going, air to breathe, and food to eat.

He gave me an approving nod. "Smart girl! And I like the analogy. We work on putting Mr. Fire on a diet by removing as much slash, snags, and deadfall as possible." He turned off the road and into a wide meadow where a helicopter and the crew waited.

"We're going to extend the firebreak at the end of this road to give Canmore protection in case a wildfire comes over that ridge." Mike pointed to a mountain covered with dark-green pines.

I scanned the ridge. "It's miles away. There'd be lots of time to put out any fire up there."

"Robin, you can't outrun a wildfire. Some move at fourteen miles per hour."

This shocked me. "So what if I'm caught in one?"

"Rule number one: Get away from the fire as fast as you can. If you're trapped on the ground, avoid any fuel sources. If possible, try to get into a lake, out from shore. If all else fails, be a gopher—dig a hole, climb in, and then cover yourself. Once the fire's passed, stay in the black, the part that's already burned, in case the wind shifts and it comes back."

I had to laugh. "It would have to be a darn big gopher hole for you to fit into."

He wiggled his eyebrows playfully. "Today should be fun. The guys are cutting the firebreak, doing rescue work, and practicing with their fire shelters. Plus handling the most important task of all—the coffee and donuts."

He parked the crew cab and I got the provisions from the backseat.

"Who's the new recruit, Mike?" One of the firefighters asked as I distributed the coffee.

"This is Robin Pearce. She's here to see what rapattackers do for fun."

"You came to the right place, Robin!" one man called.

"We're number one when it comes to shovels!" another added.

I liked the instant acceptance. For the next two hours, I watched how it was done by professionals. In full gear, complete with fire-resistant coveralls, packs, and tools, they raced to make the new firebreak. They acted as though a real fire were bearing down on them. In the smoldering summer heat, it was tough enough sitting in the shade watching. The actual chopping, shoveling, and digging must have been brutal. Even when they were dripping with sweat, they didn't complain. I guessed it would be hotter next to a real fire.

After lunch, they each practiced using a fire shelter. These tiny, fireproof tents reflect the radiant heat away from what's inside and keep people from being burned alive. The idea was that if a fire overran one of the crew, they'd crawl inside, lie facedown, and breathe the cool air closest to the ground.

"Worst-case scenario, you're trapped in a blaze," Mike explained. "Your only chance is a fire shelter, which is why my guys practice until they can deploy them in their sleep."

The crew would run for their lives, throw off all their gear, and grab their axes and fire shelters before sprinting to a cleared spot to open the tents. Mike made them do it until everyone was perfect.

Finally, it was time for the helicopter drills. This was what I'd been waiting for. I watched, enthralled, as the men climbed into the chopper and lifted off. It would hover as the crew dropped a line and then rappelled down one by one, their bright yellow jumpsuits glowing in the afternoon sun. They were something!

Mike walked over and sat beside me. "Seems easy. I don't know why those guys get paid the big bucks," he teased with his ever-ready grin.

"They're awesome!" Even I could hear the starstruck tone in my voice.

"Want to go up?"

My head whipped around. "You mean in the helicopter?"

"Unless you know another way to fly. Come on, rookie. I'll give you a crash course in helicopter etiquette, and you can go up with Vince. He's our number-one pilot."

I didn't have to be asked twice. By the time the helicopter landed, I was in a hard hat and spare jumpsuit and ready to go.

The experience was one I'll never forget. The rotor wash—the strong wind created and pushed downward by the copter's rotor blades—lashed me as I stepped on the landing rail and climbed aboard. Inside, I sat in the seat behind the crew. This was not just a drill to them. Getting it right during practice was a matter of life or death, as much as it would be during a raging wildfire. I watched as they attached their harnesses to a kind of winch called a Sky Genie, which they used to rappel down from the chopper. I was shown how it all worked. Everyone made me feel, well, grown-up and not like a punk kid asking dumb questions.

Later, as we packed up, several of the team congratulated me on a great job. This was not something I was used to from adults and it made me feel good. This was the best day I could remember in forever.

Mike drove me back to the staff quarters, and when we pulled into the parking lot, I couldn't believe what I saw.

CHAPTER SEVEN
A Different Kind of Hot

Rory sat on the wooden steps of the staff quarters. Beside his bike was my old Indian motorcycle, shining in the late afternoon sun. My excitement jumped into overdrive.

I was about to get out of the truck when Mike stopped me. "You did well today, Robin. You might think about going into this line of work. There are training classes available for bright young women like you."

"Thanks, Mike." It was something to think about in two long years, after I turned eighteen.

Rory stood as I climbed out of the truck and walked over.

"Hey, baby girl. I managed to get your bike back together and thought I'd surprise you."

I walked around the battered machine, noting the new fender, mirrors, and signal lights. "You did way more than we talked about."

"I wouldn't want the cops all over you about a stupid signal light or no mirrors. Want to take a test drive?"

"*Do I!*" I hugged him and felt his arms go around me. "I'll get my gear."

My little bike performed perfectly. The new engine note told me Rory had done some tweaking there too. Instead of her usual strangled growl, the old girl purred like a kitten.

We took the Bow Valley Parkway, and the sweet spots in the corners were particularly gratifying. When Rory turned off onto a dirt trail, I was right behind him. Our bikes snorted and bumped, scratched and jumped along the track. We even had a few mud holes to navigate. My bike was no match for Rory's monster machine, and he'd frequently have to wait while I caught up. This didn't bother him in the least, and we had a blast.

We pulled over and sat by a stream to admire the sunset.

"What do you think? Am I an ace mechanic or what?" Rory asked teasingly.

"She runs great—factory smooth!" I gave him a sidelong glance. "The question is, how much is the bill?"

He quirked his lips. "We'll figure something out. I did the work at my place, so there's no shop time owed at the garage, and as for my effort, it's negotiable." He leaned in and kissed me on the neck.

An electric current ran down my spine. I was about to say something lame, like he should do it again, when Rory reached into his leather jacket, pulled out a joint, and lit up.

I'd been around stoners before and it wasn't for me. They were so messed up, I didn't want any part of them. But this was different; this was Rory. I didn't move as he took in a lungful before offering it to me. I shook my head.

"No, thanks. I'm driving." I joked, trying to make light of the refusal.

He laughed and took another hit. "You're unbelievable. Smart and funny, all in one wickedly sexy package."

Even though it was probably the marijuana talking, his words made me tingle anyway.

"Yeah, smart, funny, and sexy. You're one lucky guy."

He held the end of the glowing cigarette to a clump of dry grass and it caught. "That's the way you make me feel." He contemplated the small blaze. "On fire."

I rubbed the smoking grass with my boot, extinguishing it. "You're pretty hot yourself."

He leaned in and his lips were warm. I felt myself responding big time. He pushed me down onto the grass and I let him. The kisses became more passionate. Time drifted as my world collapsed to a small bubble in which only Rory and I existed.

A loud peal of thunder made both of us stop. Without our noticing, the sky had grown heavy with ominous black clouds, and I could feel the wind starting to gust.

"We'd better head back. I haven't got any rain gear." I struggled to sit up, but Rory had other ideas.

"Come on, baby girl. It's a summer squall. It'll probably blow over in five minutes."

I studied the sky. "No way. It's a big one." Ducking under his arm, I stood. "We'll continue this another time. I promise."

I hoped this made him feel better. I knew guys didn't appreciate getting shut down. I also knew that riding at night, in a rainstorm, and with bald tires, was *not* fun. And Rory wasn't exactly sober. If he were in a crash now, the cops would know he was on something. The price was too steep to trade for one make-out session.

Cursing, he got up and we drove back to Banff. At the staff quarters, he waited while I parked. "Thanks for fixing my bike." I went over and kissed him, long and lingering.

"I'm impressed with how well you ride." His tone was only a little pouty.

"And I'm impressed with how well you kiss," I teased.

"You ain't seen nothin' yet." He ran his thumb along my bottom lip.

Reluctantly, I waved good-bye and walked into the lodge as the first fat raindrops hit.

CHAPTER EIGHT
Good Party

It poured all night and the wind did some serious damage. The next day the hot sun was back, drying everything out again. Work was hard, which made me doubly glad for Anne's tutoring. Slowly, I caught on to the waitress biz and my tips increased.

As I cashed out Friday, Anne came over.

"Mike's working late and I thought I'd take in the new photography exhibit at the Banff Centre. Want to come?"

The offer caught me off guard, and it must have shown on my face.

"If you aren't busy," she hastily added.

Rory had stopped by yesterday to see how the bike was running. There'd been no mention of a date, and I tried not to let it get under my skin. After the night of the storm, I was hoping for round two. I know Gran would have told me not to be too agreeable, meaning eager, and to always keep 'em wanting more, meaning that I should say no. Although she was old, Gran knew a lot about men, or more likely, she *remembered* a lot about men. I missed her and her wisdom. A lot.

"A girls' night out sounds great. Let me get cleaned up first. My perfume of hot grease and cold ketchup is gross. Want to grab a bite here before we go?"

I'd finished counting the cash drawer and took it into the walk-in freezer as I spoke. Anne stashed the tills from the bar and restaurant inside an empty hamburger-patty box in lieu of a proper safe. The restaurant had really been hopping, and there was a lot of cash, which, I was pleased to say, balanced to the penny.

Anne tilted her head. "Hmm. You've eaten here every night since you started. You must have tried everything on the menu by now. What if I take you out to supper?"

"And I'm happy to report it's all delicious." I thought about her offer. "But something different would be nice."

"There's a Mexican bar with great food on Banff Avenue," Anne said brightly, before hesitating. "Did you get your replacement ID straightened out? I know they'd card you."

I felt the ice thinning under my feet and knew I had to tread carefully. "It's coming in the mail. I'm having it sent to general delivery at the post office."

"Hmm. We'd best keep it PG rated then." Anne picked up her stack of papers. "Meet you in front of the staff residence in half an hour."

The evening turned out to be a lot of fun. We went to a Greek family restaurant owned by friends of Anne's. After an exotic meal that involved grape leaves and goat cheese, it was on to the Banff Centre, which was internationally known in the art world. I loved the photography exhibit, especially the black-and-white images of stark mountains and rocky crags.

Anne was easy to talk to and knew when to be quiet, which is just as important as knowing when to say something. We chatted about lots of things, and she never pressed when I held back. It would have been nice to tell her everything because lying to her was hard. I told myself it was for her own good. She wouldn't like Kai Hunter. Robin Pearce was much nicer, much more . . . normal. At least that's the way I made her sound.

We were on our way back to the hostel when Anne had another idea.

"If you're not doing anything on Sunday the sixteenth, do you want to come with Mike and me to a concert? It's called Mountain Rock, and it's a mix of folk and what you'd call 'real' music. You know, noisy and with lyrics no one can understand." She laughed as she parked the car. "We'll take a picnic lunch and relax. I know Mike wants to talk to you more about the rapattack work. You really impressed him, and believe me, he doesn't impress easily."

I didn't want to get too buddy-buddy; even great liars slip up. The thing was, it sounded interesting, and I'd had a good time that night. Before I knew it, I heard myself agreeing to go. "Sure, should be great." I hoped I wasn't making a huge mistake.

The next week was so busy, we had to take cash out of the till halfway through some shifts to keep the amount in the tray to a minimum. Anne had shown me how to figure each staff member's expected total, and although it took me a long time, I was able to get everyone's cash drawers to balance. I was walking across the parking lot after a particularly busy Friday when Rory drove up on his bike. I hadn't heard from him all week and had a good mind to tell him to get lost.

"You done with work?" he asked.

Rory looked so good sitting there on his powerful bike with the golden afternoon sunshine making a halo around him. He was the perfect image of a really sexy boy next door. My will of iron turned to limp spaghetti and my righteous anger vaporized.

"Yup. Done. We were slammed. It was the most money we've ever taken in. It took me forever to cash everyone out."

"Then you should kick back. There's a party at Jimbo's tonight. It's gonna be wild."

I thought of the loud music, the dope, and the booze, and something unexpected happened. Instead of being excited, I felt kind of irritated. I'd rather spend the evening alone with Rory, relaxing. I doubted he'd ever turn down a party, though. I'd been busting my butt, and maybe a crazy night out would be good for me. "Sure. Pick me up at seven."

I'd bought a cute top and was waiting for an excuse to wear it. It was a soft peach color, and the material was very sheer, with a pale-blue lace cami underneath. I knew I looked hot in it and was sure Rory would notice.

"I have something to do first. I'll meet you there, baby girl."

At first I wasn't sure I'd heard right. Finally, his words registered. He wanted me to go to some strange guy's house alone, and believe me, Jimbo was about as strange as they came. It was way across town and I'd have to take my bike to get there. I had a rule about never drinking if I was on my motorcycle. My evening would definitely not be crazy. I was annoyed, but before I could persuade him to pick me up instead, he roared away. I was left standing in the parking lot. Not happy.

I was about to stomp into the staff quarters when Anne came around the corner of the building. "Robin! Just the girl I'm after."

This was unusual. Had I screwed up? Had I forgotten something when I was cashing out?

"Relax. Your probation is definitely over, and you've done so well, I think you could open in the mornings." She held out a shiny new key.

Taking the key, I was kind of shocked and very pleased. I had been working hard, and this told me Anne had noticed. Very cool. "Opening won't be a problem. I'll be there tomorrow, bright and early."

She left, and like morning mist in the warm sun, my irritation at Rory evaporated and I felt great. The idea of celebrating instantly appealed to me.

When I got to Jimbo's, the party was already out of control. I'd taken extra care with my makeup and recombed my hair when I took off my helmet. Bright light and loud music blasted from the house. I was sure the cops would be called before the night was over.

When I walked in, I saw the girls from the party in the woods, Twila and her band of Barbies. I waved and she bobbed her head at me, then continued talking. I'm sure the ladies were discussing how to solve world hunger or global warming. As if! More likely they were talking about what color to paint their toenails next.

Feeling awkward and out of place, I stood there alone. Really uncool. If Rory didn't show soon, I'd leave.

In a corner, I spotted Kyle and Jimbo doing tequila shots as Rat poured. There were several guys cheering them on, and I recognized one of the Root Cellar staff. Rat motioned for me to join them, which was not something I wanted to do. Those guys were creepazoids. Still, they might know something about Rory. I pushed my way through the crowd.

"Do you know when Rory's showing up?" I asked Kyle between rounds.

"He's tied up," Jimbo said with a snort.

"I bet he is!" Rat agreed, and all three laughed like it was the funniest thing they'd heard in a long time.

I wondered what they meant.

Kyle threw back another shooter. He wiped his mouth on his sleeve and then fingered the sheer material of my blouse. "I'm guessing you want to party." He nudged Jimbo. "Don't you think the Injun princess should be our Miss Friendly tonight?"

Jimbo leered evilly. "She could be real friendly—with all three of us. Whaddya say, princess? Wanna go upstairs an' discuss it?"

I had started to turn away from the slimeballs when Kyle's fist snaked out and grabbed my wrist. "Don't be in such a hurry, sweet thing. Rory's busy with his latest hot-

and-sweaty, which means it's up to us to keep you entertained."

He started to pull me toward the stairs. Glancing around, I saw the other onlookers had conveniently disappeared. "Get lost, loser!" I yelled, as I wrenched my arm from Kyle's grip and backed up. Too late, I realized that Rat and Jimbo had closed in behind me.

"I can't leave you three bums alone for a minute without you hitting on my girl."

I heard Rory's voice and my stomach unclenched. I hadn't realized how tense I'd been.

Shoving past Rat and Jimbo, I leaned against Rory, never so glad to see anyone in my life. His arm went around me protectively. "Your friends are scum," I said flatly.

"I know, but they're my scum," Rory laughed. "Come on, baby girl. Let's have a drink." He led me outside to a secluded spot by the back fence.

I sat on an old bench, my scowling face radiating displeasure. The close encounter with those morons had really freaked me out.

My rule was never to drink and drive. This time, though, when Rory offered me his bottle of whiskey, I was tempted. Thankfully, common sense kicked in. "Nah. If I smack my bike up one more time, my mechanic will kill me."

"One look at you and he'd get over it," Rory said, taking in my sexy top.

"Where were you tonight?" I hoped the whine in my head didn't carry over to my voice. "Not only were those loser pigs all over me, they said you were with some girl. Were you?" Maybe I had no right to be so possessive, but when I thought of how *he'd* asked *me* to this awful party, I decided that he did owe me an explanation.

"I told you I had something to do." I could hear the annoyance in his tone. In a blink, he changed gears. "Come on, baby girl, lighten up. I came here because of you."

He wrapped his arms around me and we both knew I'd give in. "Okay," I sighed. "Next time, can we go together so I don't have to worry about the Goon Squad?"

"Sure, anything you want," he agreed, nuzzling my neck.

"Were you with a girl?" I couldn't stop myself from asking.

"You're so hot tonight, why would I waste my time with second-raters?" He continued to work magic on my neck.

This wasn't an answer, but I didn't press him. We made out until, breathless, I sat back. "Whew! Time out!" I rearranged my rumpled top. "Guess what happened at work today?"

"You said it was killer busy." Rory took another drink from the bottle.

"It was. When I counted the till trays, I couldn't believe we'd all balanced to the penny. To the penny!"

"Lots of big bucks, huh?"

"Loads. Credit is dead. Long live cash!" I laughed. "At least with the twenty-something crowd."

"You locked it up? I was never good with safe combinations. There was this job where I had to get money out of the safe and half the time I couldn't get it open. My boss thought I was an idiot."

"Thankfully, I don't have to worry about safes. We stash the cash in the walk-in freezer, and my biggest problem is remembering which cardboard box it's in." He reached for me again and I wiggled away. "Wait, you haven't heard my big news! After you left, Anne found me and I thought I was in trouble. Fortunately, that wasn't it at all. She told me I was doing such a great job, she wants me to open in the morning. She gave me a key and everything." I fumbled in my jeans pocket and produced the new key. "Pretty cool, huh?"

Rory sat up. "No kidding." He paused, grinning widely. "Wait here." He left and came back with a can of pop and a plastic cup, which he handed to me. "It's only ginger ale, not champagne, but I thought we should toast your promotion."

He raised his whiskey bottle. "Here's to you moving up in the world, baby girl. Congrats!"

I touched my cup to the bottle. "Thanks." I felt so good, I moved in closer and kissed him. He put the bottle down and returned my kiss with an even hotter one of his own. After a while, he leaned against the fence and lit up a cigarette.

"I bet the bar at the hostel was rocking too."

"Yeah, seems everyone's got loads of money to spend—everyone except me." I giggled.

"No wonder your boss gave you a promotion. You deserve it," he said with approval.

I refilled my glass from the ginger ale can as I babbled on. "You're right! I need a raise. Maybe I'll suggest it to Anne. And tips have been really great too."

We talked and Rory listened attentively to every word. He laughed at the crazy things that had happened at work and kept his arm around me. The perfect boyfriend. I must have been more tired from my long day at work or more rattled than I thought, because I was suddenly exhausted.

I yawned, feeling slightly drunk, which was ridiculous. "There's no alcohol in my pop, is there?"

"No booze at all," he assured me.

"I'm beat, Rory. I should go home before I can't ride."

"Relax. The night is young." His voice was so soft, so soothing.

I was feeling sleepy and decided I'd close my eyes for just a minute.

***

The sound of cursing woke me. Groggily, I sat up. I was in a brown recliner chair in the middle of Jimbo's living room, with the sun streaming through the window. Rory was asleep on the couch. The place was trashed. There were bottles everywhere, couples passed out on the floor, and music still blaring from someone's smartphone.

My head thumped with each beat of the music. I tried to stand and my stomach lurched. I hated hangovers.

The fog cleared and I frowned. How could I be hungover? I hadn't been drinking, had I?

I must not have had enough sleep. Stupid, stupid, stupid. Ever since I was a kid, if I didn't get eight hours a night, I was a total bear. A grizzly bear. "A grizzly bear with a thorn in its paw," as Gran used to say. The nausea was new, though.

I felt something stuck in my hair. A plastic crown, the kind from a dollar store, sat perched on my head, and there was a tinfoil scepter at my feet. I didn't remember a thing about the coronation.

Groaning, I stumbled over to Rory and shook him. "I've gotta go. I have to open the restaurant. Talk to you later."

"Yeah, yeah. Sure. See ya," he growled, rolling over.

I found my helmet and painfully made my way to my bike. The ride was torturous, as my head felt like it might fall off with every bump. Mercifully, I made it to the staff lodge without throwing up. I showered and carefully, oh so carefully, brushed my teeth without bending over the sink, as tilting in any direction made the volcano in my head erupt. Pulling on last night's jeans and a clean uniform shirt, I gingerly walked to the main building. If I was lucky, I'd be in and setting up before any of the other staff came on shift.

The police cruiser waiting in the parking lot made me stop in my tracks.

CHAPTER TEN

Inside Job

What were the cops doing here?

Anne came out of the main doors of the hostel, flanked by two RCMP officers. I froze. Were they here for me? Had I been busted?

"Robin, can you come here, please?" Anne called.

I obediently went over, feeling like I was marching to my own execution.

"Hi. What's going on?" I made myself sound bright and chipper, trying to hide the nervousness in my voice.

"Someone used a key to break into the restaurant around midnight, and the cash receipts are gone." She was very stressed. "Several of the staff have keys, and the police need to make sure none of those keys were stolen. Do you have yours?"

I remembered proudly showing Rory my key last night. I fumbled in my pocket and thanked all the party gods out there when I felt the hard metal. I pulled it out. "Yes. It's right here."

"That's the last one accounted for." Anne ran her fingers through her hair, obviously upset.

"Where were you last night, Miss . . .?" the taller officer asked, pen poised over his notebook.

"The name's Robin Pearce. I was at a party at Jimbo's, I mean Jim Watson's, until about an hour ago," I stammered.

Anne's brow arched at this admission.

"Can anyone verify you were there?" he pressed.

"Yes. My boyfriend, Rory Adams. I was with him all night, and everyone at the party saw me too. I was the one in the brown chair with the tiara and scepter." I had no idea who these magical witnesses were and hoped that if the cops checked, someone would remember the passed-out girl in the middle of the living room.

The officer wrote this down and then gave me the once-over again. "A green step-side pickup was reported leaving this parking lot late last night. Do you know who owns the truck?"

My heart sped up. I was very familiar with that particular truck, which didn't matter since I sure couldn't say anything. "No, officer, I don't." This was the truth. If I told them I'd been hit by the same pickup, it would set off a chain reaction of questions as to why I'd never reported it, where was I from, and what happened to my ID. No, I honestly didn't know who owned it, and throwing myself under the bus would do no good.

The officers told Anne they'd be in touch and left.

"This is terrible," she moaned. "There was over fifteen hundred dollars in the freezer."

I thought she was going to cry. Anne had always been kind to me, super nice and fair when she didn't have to be. I wished there was something I could do to help.

She took a deep breath. "What I don't understand is how someone got in. Only people I trust have keys. I'd better call Mike and bring him up to speed." Shaking her head, Anne went back into the hostel.

Only people she trusted. I thought about last night and was so grateful I still had my key. I went to open the restaurant.

A few gallons of coffee and a greasy BLT kept me going until my shift was finally over. I drove to Ace Auto Repairs hoping to see how Rory had made out. I wondered if he'd had as rough a day as I'd had. Parties and early-morning shifts don't mix. My tips had been good, and I thought I'd take him out for pizza and tell him about the robbery.

A big guy with a lot of dark-blue tattoos on his muscled arms and a name tag that read "Frank" stood at the counter. He looked up as I walked over.

"How's ya gettin' on?" Frank's accent was straight off a Newfoundland fishing boat.

"Is Rory here?"

"Lord Jesus, no, my girl. Said he 'ad family business and 'as gone outta town for a few days."

Family business? Rory didn't have any family, and he hadn't said anything to me about leaving.

I drove over to his place hoping to catch him before he left. The house was locked, so I waded through the weeds to the garage around back.

The garage door was locked and the side window had newspaper taped across it. I was about to leave when I noticed a corner of the paper was torn. If I stood on an empty garbage can, I could see inside.

With a lot of wobbling, I balanced on the can long enough to peek in.

The first thing I noticed was that Rory's bike was gone.

The second thing I saw made my mind whirl.

It was an old green step-side truck with a broken taillight. "Son of a . . . ," I cursed.

I remembered how cool Rory had been after the crash. He wasn't upset at the driver; in fact, he said he saw *me* take the header, implying that it was my fault. I'd been so glad the police weren't going to be involved that I'd never thought how strange this was.

Since Rory had his bike, the truck must belong to one of his roommates. Was this why he didn't get the cops when it hit me? Because he wanted to protect his sleazy friends? Those guys were dangerous in more ways than one. If they had this truck at the hostel at midnight, you could bet your boots they weren't there for a cappuccino. They were up to their bloodshot eyeballs in it.

The problem was that if I told the cops, it would be good-bye Robin Pearce and hello Kai Hunter. I might as well start learning to speak Navajo.

I had to talk to Rory.

CHAPTER ELEVEN
Tragedy and Betrayal

Sunday afternoon was a perfect day for the Mountain Rock concert. I still hadn't heard from Rory, but he wasn't a good communicator, so I cut him some slack and tried not to get ticked off.

Anne and Mike picked me up, and we sang our favorite songs as we drove to the meadow where the concert would be held.

A couple of the rock bands were really good, and I even enjoyed the folky stuff.

"This is terrific. The music, the weather, the mountains!" I gushed as I ate one of the best egg-salad sandwiches I'd ever had.

"It really helps take my mind off things," Anne said, pouring me a cup of iced tea from a thermos.

"Any word on the theft?" I asked.

"The RCMP has some leads. Sadly, even if they catch whoever did it, I probably won't get the money back." Her voice sounded strained.

"Don't worry, Anne. It could have been a lot worse," Mike assured her. "What if Robin had been cashing out alone when they broke in? No one was hurt, and we'll get by."

He patted her knee in a gesture so like the ones Gran used to make, I felt a lump in my throat. I knew love when I saw it.

Mike turned to me. "We could have used your help the past few days, Robin."

"Oh, yeah? Why?" I sipped my drink.

"The rapattack crew's been busy putting out dozens of fires in the bush, and we needed more hands. We think the fires all had a human ignition source. Careless people start fires. We even had one report of some genius leaving a campsite with the fire still burning." He sounded weary, like he'd climbed this same hill many times before. "With this heat wave, the forest is a tinderbox."

"I thought there was a fire ban on." I remembered seeing the fire danger signs with the pointer well into the red, which meant no open fires were allowed.

"There has been for weeks. The problem is that there's always some enthusiastic camper dad who wants to give his kid the full wilderness experience. They figure that one little fire won't matter and merrily have their weenie roast. A spark goes up, lands in some old-man's-beard moss hanging from a tree, and wham! I'm rappelling down a rope."

Anne was already tense, and this sent her over the edge. "Those idiots don't realize they're risking the life of a rapattack fighter because they can't be happy with a sandwich and a cold drink. Every time those guys go up in a helicopter, they risk crashing, especially in a fire when the downdrafts and wind shear are so dangerous!"

Both Mike and I stared at her. So did everyone within a ten-foot radius. Her loud outburst had been so unexpected that it drew an instant audience.

"I've got to pee." Anne jumped up and marched over to the porta-potties

"Wow! She was really upset," I commented as I watched her retreating.

Mike let out a long breath. "I'm going to tell you something, and you have to keep it between us. Deal?"

He sounded serious. "Yeah, sure."

"Anne is a damn fine pilot. She flew a chopper with the forestry service; it's how we met. We'd been married a year when my crew was sent to put out a nasty little blaze by Lake Louise. Anne was our pilot. Due to the unpredictable winds, the fire had grown a lot faster than anyone expected. We could see as soon as we came over the ridge that we'd need more than one rapattack crew, but still, we had to try. Everyone was on the ground except for Chris, the last man. Anne hovered the chopper by a rock outcrop to give him some protection from the heat. A violent gust threw the helicopter into the rocks. It crumpled like an eggshell. Chris was okay; it was Anne who took the worst of it." Mike kept his gaze on the stage, where another band was setting up. "She was medevaced out, and for a while, it was touch and go. She made it, but the baby she was two months pregnant with didn't. The miscarriage devastated her. She quit the service and vowed never to fly again. That was over a year ago."

Anne was making her way back to us, and I was about to change the subject to something cheerier when some movement at the edge of the crowd caught my attention.

I stared. It was Rory, and he wasn't alone. He was pulling a tall, blond girl along behind him. She had on a tiny neon-pink tank top, which barely covered her ample chest, and the smallest jean shorts I'd ever seen. She was giggling drunkenly as she tried to walk in stiletto heels on the soft ground. When she stumbled, Rory grabbed her, and the blond melted all over him. There was a lot of skin touching.

From the way he swayed, I could tell Rory was blasted.

I felt numb.

"Robin, are you okay?" Mike asked. "Are you sick?"

"Uh, I'm fine." My numbness was quickly replaced with anger.

This must be the girl Kyle had talked about. She wasn't all that pretty really, but there was no denying she had a killer body. Compared to her, I was a boy. I'd been stupid to think Rory would be satisfied with a girl like me. I didn't even put out.

Later that night, I lay in my bed, unable to shut off my brain.

I couldn't stop thinking about what Mike had told me about Anne. It was like something right out of a horror story. To make it through such a terrible tragedy, she had to be really strong. Anne was what Gran would have called a survivor.

Next, I mentally reran the scene with Rory and the blond. I felt betrayed, used, jealous, weepy, angry, and generally undone.

Rory and I weren't exactly a couple, and he had the right to date whoever he wanted. The problem was that I thought he wanted to date me. We were so good together.

As if this wasn't enough, the robbery kept resurfacing in my thoughts, making my mind spin.

I needed to ask Rory about the truck. Why hadn't he told me it belonged to one of his roommates, and what was it doing at the scene of the robbery?

At the party, I'd been outside with Rory. His loser friends could easily have slipped away, done the deed, stashed the truck, and returned before they were missed.

The sticky part was the key.

It was then I remembered who else had been at the party. When I'd first seen the Goon Squad doing shots, I recognized one of the onlookers. He worked at the Root Cellar. If I were a betting girl, I'd put money on his having a key! Everything was there: the key, knowledge of where the money was kept, a truck for transportation, and a party as their alibi. I needed to find out who the guy from the Root Cellar was.

If I went to the police, I'd be in the mix for sure, and the tribal police and social services would be called. I'd be finished. If I didn't talk to the cops, Anne would never know who stole her money or have even a slim chance at getting it back.

It also meant those scumbags would get away with it.

CHAPTER TWELVE
Busted!

I'm still not sure how I got through the next few days. Rory should have been back, but I hadn't heard from him. Word of the robbery had spread and he'd know by now. If he didn't care enough to talk to me about it, he could drink poison and die slowly before I went to him.

My tough attitude didn't help me sleep at night. I missed Rory and didn't know how long I could hold out.

Work ramped up, mostly because of the great weather. Banff National Park was experiencing one of the hottest, driest Augusts on record. Temperatures soared and the Alberta blue sky shimmered in the heat haze.

By Sunday, I was drained. "Can work like a pack mule" was now officially on my résumé.

I was busy delivering food to table four when Twila and her Barbies trooped in. They sat in my section, chattering like a herd of squirrels. Grabbing a handful of menus, I went to do my duty.

"Hi. We have the chef's favorite for our lunch special: Wicked Tuna Casserole. It comes with a choice of soup, salad, or fries." I distributed the menus.

Twila did a double-take right out of the movies. "Hey, aren't you Rory's Indian princess? Robin, right?"

"Yeah, that's me." I ignored the princess comment.

"We haven't seen much of you lately," Twila said, and one of her entourage, a girl with super-thick navy eyeliner and a bright-orange mouth, giggled.

"Sucks about the guys, huh?" I must have looked puzzled by her question, because she went on. "They had it coming. Honestly, they are mindless drones driven by their hormones."

Now I really was clueless, and Twila tried to help me out.

"Kyle, Rat, and Jimbo hit on the wrong Miss Friendly the night of the party. They got some cop's daughter who called her old man when the boys tried to play their stupid game with her. They were busted and charged with sexual assault. The cops hauled them off to jail." She furrowed her penciled brows. "You must have heard the racket. It was not long after they tried it with you."

I calculated the time. I arrived around seven thirty. They got stupid with me about eight, which means that the Goon Squad would have been on their way to jail well before midnight.

A mental picture of the scene formed in my mind. Whole chunks of that night were missing from my memory, and discovering which of the Root Cellar staff I'd seen at the party was proving almost impossible. I'd done some undercover snooping at work with no answers. Plus, when I ran into a party guest I recognized, I'd ask for any details they remembered. With the three losers out of the picture, the Root Cellar dude had to be the one who pulled off the robbery. Had the goons given him the truck? And how did he get it back in the garage after the robbery? The door had been locked when I'd tried it. The mysteries were piling up.

I woke late on Monday morning to a familiar rumble in the parking lot. I'd know that engine anywhere. Leaping out of bed in my shorts and T-shirt, I ran out onto the wide porch surrounding the staff quarters.

"It's about time you got up!" Rory climbed off his bike and strode toward the steps.

He had some nerve coming here without so much as a text message. "Why are you gracing me with a visit, Rory?" My Gran always said the best defense was a strong offense, and she wasn't talking about football.

"Come on, baby girl, don't be harsh. I've been out of town." He pulled his helmet off.

The image of him and the big-breasted blond popped into my head. "What happened to the skank you were with at the concert? Did she ditch you for richer pastures?"

This made Rory stop. "Who are you talking about?"

"The blond slut dressed like a cheap porn star. Don't deny it, Rory. I saw you together." I was on a roll and it felt good.

Then he did something that made me want to find a gun and borrow some bullets. He laughed.

"Are you kidding me? That was Janine. She's the girlfriend of a buddy of mine from Toronto. They were passing through and came by for a visit. Janine wanted to go to the concert, but Trevor was too loaded, so I took her."

"Come off it, Rory!" I shot back. "You were drunk or doped up—maybe both—but you sure weren't sober. And the way she draped herself all over you? Gross!"

"We're friends, that's all. I would have called, except we've been in Jasper all week. Come on, baby girl. I've missed you."

My righteous rage faltered. "Jasper?"

"Yup, Jasper. They'd never been there, so we decided to go. It was kind of spur of the moment."

"Is this the truth?" I could feel my anger evaporating.

"Would I lie to my favorite girl?" He took the steps two at a time, lifted me off my feet, and whirled me around.

I couldn't help it; I started laughing, too.

"Let's go for a ride. It's too nice a day to waste. I brought lunch to go, you know, so we could chillax." Rory indicated his bike, which was loaded with a plastic cooler, a spare gas can, and a sleeping bag.

There was a lot I wanted to talk over with him, and after hearing his explanation, I kind of owed him an apology. "Okay, I may have overreacted a tiny bit. You can't blame me, though. How was I supposed to know what was going on?"

A shadow crossed his face and his voice became steely. "I don't have to explain myself to you or anybody else!"

I stepped back, startled, and he regained control. "Today is a big day, okay? And I'm not going to let anything spoil it."

He smiled and I melted. It was so hard to stay mad at him.

"While I was in Jasper, I picked something up for you." He reached into his jacket and retrieved a small, blue-velvet bag. Untying the drawstrings, he withdrew a delicate gold pendant on a fine chain. The pendant was in the shape of a flame, a golden tongue of fire, detailed and finely crafted.

I gasped. "Oh, Rory, it's beautiful!"

"Yeah, and I got something cool to match. Kind of his and hers." He reached back into his jacket and took out a gold lighter, an exact duplicate of the pendant. With a flick of his thumb, he lit it, staring into the pillar of fire leaping from the lighter. "It's the kind that stays lit, even in a wind. When I saw this and the flame necklace, I thought of us. Well, you, really. You're on fire, baby girl." Putting his lighter away, he undid the clasp on the pendant's chain. "You'll have to take that other necklace off first."

My hand flew to my locket. "I never take this off. It was my mom's."

His face hardened. "This trinket was very pricey. I expect you to wear it."

The bossy tone irked me. I didn't want to fight, so I reluctantly took off my necklace, tucked it into the velvet pouch, and put it in my pocket. I felt alone without it, vulnerable and empty. Rory fastened his gift around my neck, and the flame flashed in the sunshine. It was stunning.

I held the pendant. It was strangely cold and I shivered. "Thanks, Rory." When I looked into his ice-blue eyes, I felt that shiver again.

It was a nice day. And I *did* have it off. "Give me twenty minutes."

CHAPTER THIRTEEN
The Man behind the Mask

The ride was one of my best ever. Rory took us far into the backcountry south of Banff. The sun was hot, and I was glad when the twisted trail took us high up the side of a mountain, where the air was not as stifling as on the valley floor. We went by a hillside crowded with reddish-brown pines, lifeless and dry.

"Pine beetles," I called over the noise of our engines. "They've killed off this whole section of the valley."

Rory hooted. "Looks *really* dried out."

We finally stopped on the edge of a high overlook with a sweeping view of the entire valley. The forest surrounded us, and I was able to gaze down at the tops of the trees growing up the slope, rich as a green velvet cape. The view was spectacular, and I fished my cell phone out.

"No coverage up here, baby girl." Rory said, unpacking his bike.

"You're right." There were no bars on the tiny scale. "The camera works fine, though, and it's pictures of this I'm after." I spread my arms to encompass the wide panorama. "Spectacular" was the only word for it. Far in the distance, I could see Mount Rundle to the east and Sulfur Mountain to the west, with Banff snuggled between them like a favorite child.

The day was a scorcher. The breeze swirling down the valley felt as hot as the air from a blast furnace. Rory laid the sleeping bag out as a picnic blanket, and we ate in the shade of a windswept pine.

When lunch was over, we sat silently watching the world go by. As my fingers toyed with the satiny label on the sleeping bag, my mind replayed those annoying questions that had kept me staring at the ceiling all night.

Rory must have sensed my agitation. "What's up? You cranked at me again?"

I thought about seeing him with the blond. Something about his explanation didn't add up. "You want me to be honest?"

"Never lie to me." Rory shook his finger at me. "No liars allowed."

He was behaving weirdly. "Okay. The chick at the concert, she wasn't your buddy's girlfriend, was she?"

I could tell he was on the edge of real anger when he answered. "You won't let that go, will you? Fine, you asked for it. She's his girlfriend, all right. But the thing is, he's back in Toronto. Janine's a hard-core party girl. We had a few laughs and spent some time in the sack. No big deal."

My heart broke at this. I remembered when Twila told me he was a player. She wasn't just telling me; she was warning me. I'd said I was okay with it. Now I had to live up to those words.

I could wish all I wanted but it wouldn't change things. Rory wasn't the kind of guy who'd settle for one girl. Since he was finally telling me straight-up what happened, maybe I could get answers to those other pesky questions.

"Why didn't you tell me that one of your friends owns the truck that hit me?"

He never missed a beat. "It was no big deal. No harm, no foul. And I fixed your lousy bike for you."

This stung. I thought he liked my old Indian.

"Come on, baby girl, let's change the subject."

Rory reached for me, but I pushed him away. I wanted answers. "Who had the pickup the night of the robbery?"

This got his attention, and he turned on me as fast as a rabid dog. "What business is it of yours?"

No surprise, no shocked denial. A bad feeling slithered up my spine. "The cops said a green step-side truck was seen leaving the hostel parking lot."

"Yeah, so?"

A light flickered in his eyes, a light I'd seen once before when a clerk had given him the wrong change. Rory went ape, yelling and cursing. I thought he was going to punch the kid.

I kept on. "I think the truck was used in the robbery. The odd thing is that, at the time it was spotted, the Goon Squad had already been run in for groping some girl. So they had to have an accomplice."

Rory took out his gold lighter and began flicking it on and off, on and off.

My mind worked through the details and everything became clear at last—the truck, the questions about cashing out, the unexplained hangover. With a flash of clarity, I knew what had happened. "I saw a guy who works at the Root Cellar hanging with those three creeps and thought he was the missing element. I figured the creepazoids supplied the truck, the staff dude supplied the key, and the party gave them all an alibi. They'd leave, steal the money, and be back before anyone knew they were gone. I tried really hard to fit all this together so it made sense."

He flicked his lighter again.

"Rory, have you ever heard of Occam's razor?"

"Can't say I have." His voice had that edge again.

"It basically means that the simplest explanation is usually the right one. You know, if it walks like a duck and quacks like a duck, it's probably a duck. Don't go looking for elephants."

"What the hell are you talking about?" he snapped.

"I made up this complex scenario with the Goon Squad and the staff guy in on it together, lots of cloak-and-dagger stuff. What a load of crap."

"Where are you going with this, Robin?"

"I was right about one thing. The person with the key was at the party." I took a deep breath. "It was me. I supplied the key and the information. You did the rest."

My stomach tightened when I thought of how Anne had trusted me. "The morning after the party, I felt so hungover, but I hadn't been drinking, so I chalked it up to not getting enough sleep. The thing is, that wasn't my first rodeo. I've been to some nasty bashes and know what a roofie is. It's called 'the forget pill.' You drugged me, Rory. You put Rohypnol in my drink, and when I passed out, you took my key. You used the truck so if anyone saw it, the goons would be blamed, and who would believe them when they claimed to be innocent? After robbing the hostel, you returned the truck to the garage and came back to the party. On your fast bike, you weren't gone long, and staying with me until morning made me your alibi, just like you were mine. I was so out of it, you could have asked me to take a ride on a flying carpet and I'd have bought a ticket."

"You're not as dumb as you seem." His words were carved from ice.

"You must have freaked when you discovered your three friends had been picked up by the cops. Kinda shot down your plan to have them take the fall." I turned to him. "Rory, why'd you do it?"

"How could I pass on a sweet deal like that? All I had to do was get you to cooperate. The problem was, you're such a goody-goody, you'd never have gone along with my plan. I had to put you out of action while making you believe we were together all night in case the cops asked. I was just going to get you drunk, and it would have worked, except for your stupid rule about not drinking when you're on your bike. Something else was called for. I always carry some 'persuader' with me in case my dates are uncooperative. Once you were out of it, things got simple."

I was shocked and disgusted. He was a monster. Rory clicked the lighter again and gazed into the flame. There was something about his expression that scared me. If I were to draw a picture of pure evil, that look on his face would be my model.

Watching him, hypnotized by the flame, another bell chimed in my brain. I remembered Mike talking about a truck leaving the scene of one of the wildfires. "Oh my God. There's been a rash of wildfires and the forestry service thinks careless campers are accidentally starting them. But that's not true. You're starting the fires!"

"Right again, baby girl. That's why I can't stay too long in one place. Eventually someone would put it together; I show up and fires happen. Buildings burn, cars explode, houses mysteriously go up in a blaze of glory. Fire is magic. It's so . . . alive." He chuckled, a sound like teeth scraping on bones. "When I heard you'd been questioning everyone about the night of the robbery, I knew my time here was done. It was a totally disloyal thing to do and you'll pay for your crime, Robin."

"Is that why you bought me the flame necklace? Because you get off on fire?"

"Who said I bought it? I said I *picked it up* for you. It's too bad you aren't more into this, then you'd truly enjoy what I've got in mind for this afternoon's entertainment."

The guy I was seeing now was a stranger. He was insane, and I had no idea what he was going to do next. Glancing around, I gauged the best way out of there.

"I'm going to give Banff something to remember me by." He got up and walked to his motorcycle. "I'm such a good Boy Scout, I came prepared!" He picked up the can of gasoline he'd brought and must have seen the alarm on my face. "I bet you thought this was in case we ran out of juice for our bikes. Wrong! I figure with this wind, the fire should funnel down the valley like a red-hot tsunami. You noticed the dead pines we rode through on our way here? Each one is like a stick of dynamite."

I was terrified now. "You're not serious, are you?"

"Don't worry, we'll be long gone. I've got plans for us. You and I are going to spread fire from coast to coast. You're my flame, baby girl."

As I watched, he undid the cap on the gasoline can.

"Rory, don't do this," I pleaded. "I'll go with you. Sure, we can travel together, you and me. Just put the gas down! No fires, okay?"

"You don't understand, baby girl. You going with me isn't optional. We're a team now." He poured the volatile liquid onto the trees below the cliff edge where we'd eaten our lunch. The smell of gasoline filled the air.

I glanced at my bike. If I could make it back to Banff, I could warn . . . warn who? Who'd believe I wasn't in on it? A runaway teen who parties with a wild bunch and whose boyfriend is a thief and a pyromaniac?

I thought of Mike and Anne and how much I liked them. They were what Gran called salt-of-the-earth folks. I'd messed up with Rory and he'd taken advantage of me. He had to be stopped before he turned this place into an inferno.

I ran at Rory. Hitting him hard, I shoved him toward the edge of the cliff. The wind exploded out of his lungs as I drove him backward.

He stumbled before regaining his balance. I'd underestimated his strength. He dropped the gas can and lunged for me, screaming his rage. "I'll kill you, you worthless bitch!"

I kneed him as hard as I could in the groin, and he roared again. Grabbing my hair, he snapped my head back.

Pain hit me like a hammer blow, but still I didn't give up. I couldn't. Too much was riding on my stopping him. I drove my elbow into his solar plexus. He buckled and let go.

Stumbling, Rory teetered on the edge of the cliff, his arms windmilling as he tried unsuccessfully to regain his balance.

I saw him fall. I heard him scream. All that remained afterward was silence.

It was a long way down to the valley floor. Rory couldn't have survived the fall. Slowly, I walked to the edge of the cliff. Steeling myself, I peered over.

Twenty feet below, a rocky shelf jutted out from the cliff. Rory lay sprawled on the ledge, one leg twisted at a grotesque angle. This was the guy I'd fantasized about and thought was so cool. How could I have been so blind? I stared down at his crumpled body.

Suddenly, Rory opened his eyes!

Slowly, his mouth gaped and a bloody gash grinned up at me. I saw his hand move to his pocket as he took out his golden lighter.

"Did you think it was over, baby girl?" he rasped. "I've always wanted to be inside it, watching, enjoying the total destruction. Soon, the beast will eat this whole valley!"

The lighter flared to life and with a strangled laugh, Rory dropped the torch into the gasoline-soaked pines far below.

"Noooo!" My scream echoed off the rock walls as the lighter gracefully arced toward the waiting trees.

With a loud *whoosh!* the pines exploded into flame. The fire leaped up the trees, hungrily devouring the branches in bursts of bright light and instant heat.

In seconds, the fire gained strength. Rory had been right; it seemed eerily alive! Trees blazed as the fire jumped from one pine to the next. The wind grabbed the smoke, swirling it into fantastic shapes of black, gray, and an ugly, bruised-looking purple.

The fire sped down the hill, following the trail of gasoline. The wall of flame raced toward the area devastated by the pine beetles. Those dead trees were like bombs waiting to explode.

Unexpectedly, something strange happened. The wind changed direction.

The fire now clawed its way back up the hill toward us. Within minutes, we'd be engulfed! I saw Rory on the ledge below, his eyes dancing as he watched the flames.

Mike's words crowded into my head.

Rule number one: Get away from the fire as fast as you can. My bike was waiting, but I couldn't leave Rory to be burned alive. The thought made me sick. Even he didn't deserve to die like that.

Next: Find a zone with no fuel. Impossible! We were surrounded by trees.

Maybe I could submerge myself in a lake? I'd noticed water seeping out a rock face nearby. But that was no good; it was too little.

I also remembered what Mike said about updrafts. They burn faster than fires moving downhill. The canyon below, like a chimney, would create an updraft.

Faster and faster, the wildfire raced up the hill toward us. There was very little time left.

The day I'd gone with the rapattack crews, I'd watched them practice with their fire shelters. Was there anything I could use to rig one now?

Searching the picnic site, I didn't see anything. Then I spotted our leather jackets and the sleeping bag. I bundled them up and took them to the small pool of water I'd seen below the seepage from the rock wall. While they were soaking up the water, I moved my motorcycle into the clearing, as far from the trees as possible. No way would I abandon the old girl without a fight, even if the odds were stacked against her.

I was about to go for the jackets and sleeping bag when I thought of something else Mike had said. "If all else fails, be a gopher. Dig a hole and climb in."

I grabbed a screwdriver from the small tool bag strapped behind the seat of my bike.

Unfortunately, when I picked up the jackets and sleeping bag, they weren't so much soaking wet as mildly damp. It would have to do. Thick, choking smoke made it hard to breathe as I ran to the cliff's edge.

Throwing the jackets and sleeping bag off the cliff, I was happy to see them land beside Rory. Carefully, I shinnied over the edge and worked my way down the steep rock face. I'd almost reached the bottom when my foot slipped and I lost my grip.

I felt myself falling but didn't have the breath to scream.

With a bone-jarring thump, I landed on the rocky shelf. Scrambling over to Rory, I scratched at the thin layer of earth with my screwdriver, making a shallow depression.

"We're going to burn, burn, burn!" Rory said gleefully.

He sounded insane. "Not if I can help it!" I said through gritted teeth.

I rolled him into the shallow trench, face down, and got in beside him. Pulling the wet sleeping bag and leather jackets over us, I put my face in the dirt and prayed.

The fire roared over us like a freight train. The heat was unbearable, and I imagined my skin blistering. I was sure we'd explode into flame, just like the trees I'd watched moments earlier. Choking, I tried to breathe, but the air seared my lungs. Ashes filled my mouth. Our leather jackets gave some protection, and I remembered seeing something on the sleeping-bag label about it being fire retardant.

Agonizing minutes crawled by as the fire incinerated everything around us. I kept praying.

Finally, the noise lessened. The heat was still so intense; I waited precious minutes longer before daring to lift the edge of my jacket to peer out.

Blackened spires were all that was left of the beautiful pines. The fire was now burning its way up the mountain. As I watched the embers rise high into the sky and fall, I knew we weren't out of danger yet. All it would take was one of those sparks to hit the dead pines below and the whole thing would start over again.

"Are you okay?" I asked, not sure if Rory had made it.

He groaned as I threw off the smoldering jackets and scorched sleeping bag. His leg was still twisted awkwardly, and I knew it was badly broken.

With no cell phone coverage, there was only one thing to do.

"I'm going for help." As I struggled to my feet, Rory gripped my arm.

"You can't leave me here!" he shrieked. "What if it comes back?"

I wrenched myself free. "Well, I guess you'll have a front row seat to your handiwork."

Scrabbling up the cliff, I fought my way to the top.

The first thing I saw was my little Indian, untouched, sitting there surrounded by ashes. It was as if the old girl had been caught in an unexpected snowstorm.

Running to the bike, I crossed my fingers. I turned the key, cranked the kick starter, and as if by a miracle, the old girl started! Whooping for joy, I spun out of there and began the long ride to Banff.

Mike's words, "stay in the black," came back to me. Stay in the area already burned. I figured that wouldn't be too hard since the whole place was toast.

Rounding a corner, I skidded to a stop. The road was blocked by downed trees, still smoking. I'd been on the same road years ago and remembered a shortcut I'd used. With any luck, it was still passable. If I were caught on those trails, there'd be no way out. I took a deep breath and headed into the brush.

The detour was grueling, and it was a miracle I made it through. It dumped me out not far from Banff. The first place I went was the hostel. I needed Mike, and Anne would know where to find him.

Racing into the main building, I barged into the office. "Anne, I need Mike. There's . . ." My words trailed off. They were both sitting and having coffee.

Mike took one look at me, scorched and sooty, and leaped to his feet. "Where?"

"South of town, past the Goat Creek Trail, near the Spray Lakes turnoff."

"I'll call dispatch and get a crew out there." He picked up the phone and dialed.

"Are you all right?" Anne asked, wrapping her arms around me.

"I'm fine. It's Rory. I left him back there. He's got a broken leg." The tears started before I had a chance to stop them. "Anne, he started the fire. He's been starting all the fires, and he stole the money!"

Mike put the phone down with a slam. "The crews were assigned to a wildfire near Jasper. They're on their way back in the big helicopter, but it will take a while. Robin, can you take me to the fire?"

I thought of my old Indian. "It will be slow with two riders." My throat tightened as I spoke. "There's a stand of dead trees not far from Rory, and if the wind shifts . . . Mike, it was terrible. I made a fire shelter and it blazed over us. I was sure we were going to die."

Mike turned to Anne. "We have to get him out. The small chopper is at the heliport. We could take it."

Anne shook her head, desperation in her voice. "No, Mike, don't ask me, please."

He gently took her hands in his. "Robin's right. If the fire circles back, we'll have a major blaze to deal with. If I can get up there, I can cut a firebreak. Vince and the crew will be here in two hours, but we can't wait. A lot can happen in a couple of hours."

"I haven't flown in over a year, and you know why," Anne argued.

I had to say something. "Rory's not a good guy, Anne, but he has mental problems, real ones, and needs help. We can't leave him to die."

She hesitated. "If I'm flying the chopper, who's going to rescue this boy?"

Good question. With Mike working the firebreak, there was only one other person who could do it. I thought of dangling from the underside of a helicopter and all the things that could go wrong. Then I remembered the fire and how terrified I'd been of being burned alive. Rory might be facing that horror right now. "I can do it. I had a lesson from the rapattack crew and know all the basics." This was what Gran would have called a fat white lie.

I thought Anne was going to say no again. Instead, something shifted, and she smiled. A small smile, but a smile nonetheless. "Let's go."

It was a tight squeeze to get all of us in the little helicopter, especially with Mike's gear. There was a modified Sky Genie winch, and Mike showed me how it worked. It was simple and I knew it wouldn't be a problem to operate.

Piloting a helicopter must be the same as riding a bicycle, because Anne had no trouble remembering how to operate the machine and we were soon up and away.

As we neared the fire, I could see it was confined to the valley behind the rocky point that Rory and I had picnicked on. "The road's cut off below us," I yelled over the noise of the engine and pointed.

Mike radioed this information to the base for the incoming crews to use. "From the direction of the smoke, the wind is driving the fire up the gorge and away from the stand of dead pines. We might get lucky and trap it between the burned area and my firebreak. It will cut off the fuel supply." He motioned past the spikes of flame flaring through the smoke. "Anne, put me down on that cut line."

She nodded and landed the little helicopter smack in the middle of the cleared area as easily as she would park her car at the mall. Mike leaned over me and gave his wife a swift kiss. "Good luck."

Anne appeared calm, too calm, and I suspected what was going through her mind. She needed to stay in the present, so I tried to distract her.

"Do you think the winch will be able to hoist Rory and me both up at once?"

She refocused. "What? Oh, the winch? It'll be maxed but will work. The trick's going to be keeping this jumpy thing steady."

When we got to the ledge, Anne hovered the small helicopter. I could see Rory lying on the ground, not moving.

"The winds are unpredictable, Robin. Go as fast as you can."

The warning in Anne's voice was clear. I checked my harness and stepped out onto the landing rail. The wind whipped my face as panic squeezed me, like a python wrapped around my chest. I ignored it and activated the winch.

Swaying beneath the helicopter, I twisted and turned. Anne maneuvered to give me the safest landing possible. This meant moving close to the cliff face. I couldn't imagine the skill and willpower it must have taken to do this. A burst of affection for this amazing woman made me realize how much I cared for her. I wished Gran could have met Anne. They'd have liked each other instantly.

The second my feet touched down, I unhooked the winch clip, ran to Rory, and buckled a harness on him. He screamed when I moved his leg, and he picked up a sizable rock. "Get away from me! We'll both die on that thing!"

My patience was done with Mr. Rory Adams. "We don't have time for your drama-king act!" I growled, and slapped him across the face.

His mouth fell open. "You hit me!"

"Yes, and I'll do it again if you don't shut up!"

He shut up.

I clipped the winch to our harnesses and pressed the switch to bring us back up to the helicopter. There was a hard gust of wind and the chopper swerved and dipped. We swung wildly out over the gorge, and my stomach leaped into my throat. Rory clung to me, and this time, I clung back.

Groaning under the strain, the winch finally stopped at the open door to the helicopter, and I shoved Rory inside. "Unhook your harness!" I yelled, my feet balancing precariously on the landing rail.

He did and I clambered up beside him, undoing my own winch clip. I was never so glad to be squished into an uncomfortable seat with a sweaty, smelly, sooty guy in my life. Rory was pale and shaky. "Relax. We made it!" I tried to comfort him.

Anne glanced over and handed me an airsickness bag.

"It's okay. I feel fine," I protested, then Rory heaved and I was glad I had the bag.

CHAPTER SIXTEEN
Home and Dry

Anne flew directly to Canmore Hospital, and they took Rory into surgery for his fractured leg. While Anne filled in the paperwork, I told her everything I knew about my ex-boyfriend and what he'd been up to.

"The police should be called."

Anne took out her cell phone, and I swallowed nervously. "Do you think I'll have to talk to them too?"

"Don't worry. You haven't done anything wrong, have you?" Anne asked pointedly.

"I didn't have anything to do with Rory's stupidity. Honest." No, I thought, I had enough stupidity of my own.

I reached for the flame pendant and discovered it was gone. The chain must have broken during the rescue. Whichever bear, cougar, or moose found it, they could keep it! That thing had felt wrong since the beginning.

I pulled the blue pouch from the pocket of my jeans and put my own locket back on, knowing I'd never take it off again. I felt stronger with it on, and with the way I'd screwed up the last few weeks, I'd need all the strength I could get to face the future.

We went back to the hostel and were surprised later when Mike walked into the restaurant.

"There are my girls!" He greeted us cheerily, his face black with soot and his clothes reeking of smoke. "I stopped at the hospital, and you'll be happy to know the police were busily charging Rory with multiple crimes."

"Are you okay?" Anne asked anxiously.

"I'm fine, and I have some great news, ladies. The fire's contained and on its way to being out, thanks to you and Robin." His voice became serious. "Anne, if you hadn't flown me there so quickly, it might not have turned out so well. I know what it took for you to get back into a helicopter. Thank you, sweetheart." He pulled his hand out from behind his back and offered her a bunch of wildflowers, only slightly singed.

She took the flowers, sniffing them appreciatively. "Maybe it's time we talked about me flying again. Since I have such a competent staff now, I can leave the place and know everything will be taken care of properly."

They both smiled at me, and I was about to say something when I glanced past Mike and saw two RCMP officers striding toward us. It was the same two I'd met the morning after the robbery. I remembered the way the big guy had scrutinized me, filing my face in his own personal database. They weren't delivering good news.

"Kai Hunter?" the big one asked.

The jig was up and I was tired of lying. "Yes, I'm Kai Hunter. Please don't take me back! There's nothing left for me on the reservation. My Gran was all I had, and she's gone." I was pleading.

The constable wasn't sympathetic. "You'll have to come with us. Social services is waiting to take you into custody. A sixteen-year-old alone on the streets won't last long."

"Officer," Anne interrupted, "she's not alone and she's not on the streets. I suspected she was underage and made sure she was taken care of and supervised, or at least as supervised as possible."

I frowned, confused. "How—"

Anne shook her head as if to say, "nice try, but it ain't gonna fly."

"Robin, or should I say Kai, you're not a good liar. When you arrived, you said you didn't have any ID because your wallet was stolen, but you had your wallet. You put those twenties back in it when I was taking you to the staff quarters. The tribal police visited not long after you came and asked about a runaway with a distinctive dragonfly tattoo on her wrist. I had a hunch what was under your bandage. I decided to watch over you until you trusted me enough to explain what was going on."

"I do trust you!" I protested. "Both of you!" My eyes swept desperately from Anne to Mike. "I'm sorry I lied. I was going to tell you, except I thought it would screw everything up. I don't want to learn Navajo!"

They exchanged an intense look, and it was as if some mental message passed between them. Anne put her hand gently on my shoulder.

"Kai, in the past you've made some bad choices." Her tone was stern, and I dreaded what was coming next. "We want to help you make better ones in the future."

Mike stepped forward and addressed the policemen. "We'll speak to social services about fostering Kai. She'll live with us, and we'll make sure she goes to school, eats her vegetables, and doesn't stay out too late. We'll also make sure she stays in touch with her First Nation's roots. We'll take her to visit the elders on the reserve and go to as many powwows as she wants."

My heart knew this was so right. Gran would want me to stay connected to my culture, and truthfully, I wanted it too. I was proud to be Indian. We rocked!

Mike's next words made me stop breathing for a minute.

"Then, if she decides we pass muster, we'll apply to formally adopt her. That is, if Kai wants us to."

They turned to me, waiting.

"Me? Live with you? Here?" I couldn't believe it.

"Actually, you should move into our house. There's a room waiting." Anne brushed a lock of my garish hair out of my eyes. "We both want you to stay."

"And I can help with your application for firefighting school when you turn eighteen. You're a shoo-in," Mike added with a wink.

The RCMP officers were speechless, something I'd never seen before. And this was, after all, not my first rodeo.

I imagined what it would be like to have Anne and Mike for parents. "I'd like that. A lot." I smiled.

All at once we were talking, hugging, and laughing, and when I listened closely, I thought I could hear Gran laughing too.

I was home.

Resources

United States

1-800-RUNAWAY (1-800-786-2929)

Call this hotline if you're a teenager who's thinking of running away from home or know someone who is, you have a friend who has run and is seeking help, or you are a runaway ready to go home.

nationalsafeplace.org

Safe Place is a national youth outreach program that educates thousands of young people every year about the dangers of running away or trying to resolve difficult, threatening situations on their own. The 24-hour crisis line has an experienced frontline team of members ready to help. If you're not ready to call, you can post to the bulletin board, send an email, or start a live chat. It's anonymous, confidential, and free.

TXT 4 HELP

TXT 4 HELP is a nationwide 24-hour text-support service for teens in crisis. If you're in trouble or need immediate help, text "safe" and your current location (address/city/state) to 69866. Within seconds you'll

receive a message with the closest Safe Place location
and contact number for the local youth shelter. You
will then have the option to text interactively with a
mental health professional for more help. It's quick,
confidential, and safe.

teen.fightforzero.org
hotline@fightforzero.org
724-656-STOP
Fight for Zero works to stop sexual assault, date rape,
and domestic violence and provides help and support
for teens, parents, and schools.

Canada
kidshelpphone.ca
1-800-668-6868
Kids Help Phone offers free, 24/7, anonymous,
confidential, and nonjudgmental phone counseling and
web counseling for anyone age twenty and younger.

Canada Hotlines
Crisis Intervention Centre: 1-800-757-7766
Parents Help Line: 1-888-603-9100
Sexual Assault Support and Crisis: 1-800-909-7007
S.O.S. Femmes: 1-800-387-8603

About the Author

Jacqueline Guest is a Métis writer who lives in a log cabin nestled in the pinewoods of the Rocky Mountain foothills of Alberta, Canada. She is the current Creator in Residence for the Canadian Society of Children's Authors, Illustrators, and Performers and the proud recipient of the 2013 Indspire Award for the Arts. Her award-winning books feature main characters from different ethnic backgrounds, including First Nations, Inuit, and Métis. Her well-drawn characters face issues common to every young person, such as bullying, blended families, and physical challenges, providing strong role models for today's youth.

7th GENERATION

PathFinders novels offer exciting contemporary and historical stories featuring Native teens and written by Native authors.

For more information, visit:
NativeVoicesBooks.com

No Name
Tim Tingle
978-1-939053-06-0 • $9.95

Tribal Journey
Gary Robinson
978-1-939053-01-5 • $9.95

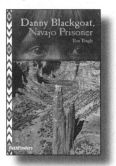

**Danny Blackgoat,
Navajo Prisoner**
Tim Tingle
978-1-939053-03-9 • $9.95

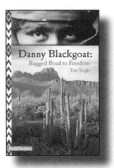

**Danny Blackgoat:
Rugged Road to Freedom**
Tim Tingle
978-1-939053-05-3 • $9.95

Available from your local bookstore or you can buy them directly from:

Book Publishing Company • P.O. Box 99 • Summertown, TN 38483
888-260-8458

Please include $3.95 per book for shipping and handling.